# PROJECT RECYCLE

# PROJECT RECYCLE
## Sharne Williams

**TAMARiND HiLL**

**.PRESS**

Dedicated to Ariel;

may we all find the courage to live in our truth

# THE ASSIGNMENT

At the prime age of 27; my 28th birthday just around the corner, I was forced to sit back and take a long look at my life.  One failed marriage, two broken engagements, eight steady girlfriends, four affairs, about nine flings and a few one night stands later; I am single, a status I had not claimed since the very tender age of 15. Were it not for the attempt on my life by my fucking mad ex-wife, I probably would have just carried on without paying attention to all of this.

Like you, I might not have realised that this had been my life. I'd never really taken stock and the moment I began at the god damn recommendation of my £80.00 an hour therapist, I started to realise that everything had just passed me by because for some reason I was just not present. This 'memoir', if I may even call it that is not really about the stock taking; it is more about the mistakes I had to face the moment I started 'taking stock' at my therapist's requests.

After visiting her for almost three whole months and barely making conversations, you know; 'letting her in', I finally decided to give it a go. "Just talk to her, see if she can figure out why you feel so fucked up inside, so damn crippled", I told myself. So, I gave it ago. In the beginning, we talked about my childhood and the horrible relationship with my mother. How I emancipated myself from her for fear of her ruining my life as she had done hers. How I escaped her; I didn't want to become the lady who lives with her daughter in the two up two down, every man in town knew her address and had been in her house at some point in time to do whatever it is they did in her bedroom. No, I wanted to be someone else, but I soon realised I had become what I feared the most.

I never had a stable relationship and all the women who I'd dated had lost my very fickle love, as soon as I had latched on to the next best girl that caught my eye. 'She stimulates my intellect', I'd tell myself. Then, before you know it I was in her bed or she was in mine or wherever the heat had gotten hold of us, be it in an alleyway, the bathroom of a restaurant or once even in an airport during transit. Yes, I had become my mother. I suppose my sex drive was inherited. It must have been.

So, as time went by and we unpacked my many issues with my therapist; who I must mention was quite a distraction in this process, I realised I probably should have chosen a male therapist; someone I would have no sexual attraction to, but it was too late. I was stuck with her and a part of going to the sessions, being able to dissect my issues was the benefit of seeing her. Having been single at the time for the very first time in my life, it was a very scary place to be. I'm the kind of girl that likes companionship and I genuinely do. I like lying next to someone at nights being wrapped up in their arms or them in mine. I enjoyed the constant of a woman's scent and the gentleness in her touches. Simply put, I was not meant to be single. Before you knew it, I had my therapist laid on her desk, its contents now a mess on the floor and without shame I devoured her, and she'd let me.

But let's focus, this is not about the fact that I had become my therapist's mistress. It's about the fact that she thought I needed healing and that I could only heal by righting the wrongs in my life and forgive myself for all the wrongs I had done. Her suggestion? I should write a letter to my exes and try to resolve the unresolved issues between us. In her defence, she didn't want me to deliver them; she merely wanted me to write the letters and burn them. Well, this didn't end well, at least not for me. Writing these letters meant I had to look back at all my relationships, look at how they had impacted my life, how they had affected my behaviour. It meant that I had to dissect everything; every bit of intimacy, every lie I had told, every time I had betrayed someone's trust. Yes, it meant that I had to write about how they had hurt me and think about how I had hurt them and try to apologise. I tried. The hardest part of this? Every darn bit of it.

* * * * *

I had left the US as soon as I'd hit eighteen to move across the world with a girlfriend and to escape my mother completely. Looking back, I suppose I could have just left New York. Unfortunately or fortunately, there's no way to turn back time and I also don't think that I would.

I had lived in seven different countries and had made my last stop in central London when I married the woman of my dreams. Now that's a joke and a half right there. I had picked, picked and ended up with rubbish. I reckon this was the biggest mistake of my life, but I'll expound on that in just a moment.

Anyway, I had letters to write and in doing so I had to rehash old emotions. I suppose it was guilt; the fact that I knew I had done a lot of these women wrong, but I was only looking at the good in them. I couldn't for the life of me look at the reasons I had left or whether they had caused me pain. My letters were laced with apologies and begged for forgiveness. I hoped that I had not ruined their lives and that they had found it in their hearts to allow themselves to love again. "You deserve to be happy", I'd said in all of them. At the moment, they were good women whose lives I had ruined. I suppose I had to have come to that conclusion because I didn't remain friends with any of them. Their parting words were often "I want nothing to do with you!", and that's all I could remember. So, yes, I suppose it had to have been me. I might have actually ruined their lives and they'd never love again or let anyone in.

I wrote my letter, 14 to be exact, and I soon decided to contact some of my exes and apologise. In choosing who to address first, I wanted to write to the ones I had hurt the most, the ones who I was sure that possibly loved me. I wanted to write to the ones who I thought that for one instant that maybe had it not been for me, we could have made it. Against the orders of my therapist, by that time full on lover, I decided to seek them out and get in touch. I suppose I didn't want to listen to my therapist because I convinced myself that I could no longer trust her judgement as I thought it was clouded by our moments of passion in her office or in her bed, while her husband was travelling. I was convinced she wanted me to herself and was worried that she would have competition if one of my exes responded to my letter positively.

I had every right to think that. I never called or messaged outside of our sessions and the moments we shared would only happen when I met her for therapy, but on one occasion she dropped a massive bomb on me about wanting to leave her husband. I wasn't in love with her or looking to get into a relationship. I sometimes think I did not even see her; you know what I mean? I didn't know her likes and dislikes, I knew almost nothing about her. It was a case of sharing a gaze too long, that turned into something more and kept turning into something more, which did not include audible communication outside of "yes, yes, yes!", "don't stop I'm coming", "yes, right there" or some variation of that. It was simple, she was helping me through a very difficult time. She knew almost everything about me, I nothing about her and we had sex: passionate but no strings attached sex. That was it, at least on my part. I couldn't offer

her more, because I never even stopped to think
of her outside of sex or our sessions.

# Girlfriend No.1

Her name was Pricilla. I nicknamed her Blondie because she was a brunette with blonde pubic hair. At only 15 years old, I thought this super weird and as I had no other nickname for her that everyone else didn't call her by outside of "Baby" "sweetie" or something just as cliched, I decided to call her my Blondie. I had to write to her first because I had messed with her life big time. We dated for a mere four months, but it was such a dangerous game that I didn't even realise the danger I was putting her in.

The thing is, Blondie was grown. She was ten years my senior, yes you read right, and she thought I was nineteen. I met her at my friend's 21st birthday party. I hung around older girls and boys, more like men and women, because I thought them more on my intellectual level. Kids my age bored me to death. They offered no depth, no insight into the real issues of life. I didn't want to talk about going to the mall or the latest boy band and which Hollywood stars were breaking or making up; I needed stimulation. My friend Anna thought I was nineteen too. We met at a book club and we had forged an instant friendship. I understood entirely why she also felt betrayed when she found out I was only fifteen and wanted nothing to do with me.

Blondie and I became an item almost instantly. After a bit of conversation about my supposed pursuing a law degree at Colombia University, she was wooed, and before the party ended, we were an item. She was my first. I had fallen in love with her. Completely besotted with the beauty of her mind. She was an accountant, recently qualified, and she had the brains. She was passionate about life and wanted so much for herself. She had big dreams and she wanted so much with me. Things I'd never be able to offer her. I was merely a teenager. I didn't live in a dorm room on campus as I had told her. I lived with my madly annoying mother who drove me crazy and I was running away from her and ruining myself.

I knew what I was doing was wrong, but I felt loved by another human being and I wanted to hold on to that for as long as I could. Being in school and unable to respond to her calls wasn't too hard, as I could always make the excuse that I was in lectures. Mother dearest never knew when I was home or not, so subsequently sleeping over in her one-bedroom apartment near Time Square wasn't an issue.

She invited me over the same night we met and even though it was my first time, with me being half drunk and half asleep, it was special. I connected with her on a level I had only learned existed then and I wanted it to last. Blondie never believed it was my first time though.

'You are far more experienced than anyone I have been with. How many girlfriends have you had?" she'd questioned when we laid naked on her living room floor.

"Just you." It slipped from my lips.

"Girl come on, a girl as beautiful," she paused to kiss my lips, "as sexy", she kissed me again cupping my right breast, "as amazing as you have never been single a day in your life."

"I'm just a regular girl," I threw her on her back, climbed atop her and continued to make love to her.

I'm not sure where I had learned any of it. I'd never even watched a pornographic movie in my life; it just came naturally. At first, I suppose I matched her every move then somehow it just flowed.

* * * * *

It was all going so well, we spent every possible moment together for the few months we were together. My mother was too caught up with herself to realise I had not been spending any time at home. Then, it all crumbled when she asked me to move in with her.

I would have, but I imagined my mother would wake up one day and suddenly think of me, wouldn't find me, then she would tell the police I'm missing. Not that she'd be able to say when last she'd seen me, but either way, I didn't want to walk into the supermarket with Blondie and suddenly see my face on a milk carton with my date of birth or age on it. I just couldn't bear the thought.

Although I convinced her I couldn't move in, she still wanted me to spend most of the time with her. I tried to get out of it by convincing her that I wouldn't make my morning classes, but she insisted we could make it work. With my head somewhat screwed on, I told her I couldn't move in. I tried to make up for it by spending as much time with her as possible. I'd stay at hers up to two consecutive nights at a time, making sure not to be missing for too long. Most days my mother wouldn't even realise I hadn't been home.

Nonetheless, the thought of my face on a carton box provided enough reason to not stay away for more than two days at a time. Yet with all the care I was taking, in a matter of moments, my world was torn apart.

We were on the subway, wrapped up in each other, my hand caressing her thigh as she held my face in both her palms and kissed me; when my godforsaken Physics teacher rocked up.

"What's going on here," she snapped, pulling Blondie away from me. "Do you know that this is inappropriate behaviour for children? How dare you!"

"What's your problem lady?" Pricilla questioned.

I didn't know what to do, my knees buckled under me and I buried my face in my lap. Then, as if the universe reached out its hand to me, we came to a stop and I found the strength to run out of the train, up the stairs and out of the subway. I ran until I was all the way home. I was soaked from sweat when I got home, completely out of breath. I collapsed on my bed and cried. All I could think of was the trouble she was in. I searched myself for my mobile phone and couldn't find it and I was relieved, because there was no way for her to get in touch with me and I was glad. I didn't know what I would say to her or what she'd do. It was a major fuck up and for the first time since meeting her, I was brought back to reality. I was a kid! I was a godforsaken child!

It was Anna who brought the house down though. For some reason when she called the following week and invited me over, I didn't think that she'd spoken to Pricilla. I turned up at her house, my heart broken but a smile on my face as if to hide my pain, but it wasn't long until everything I was feeling came to light. We sat in her den, the whole time I was thinking of the heartbreak I had left Pricilla with and the trouble I had caused. Then out of nowhere, she appeared. She was standing right there in front of me.

"You talk to her, I can't stand the sight of her. It's been the most gruelling few minutes of my life having to sit here." She barely gazed at me as she left the room, but I could see the scorn and hear it in her voice. She knew.

"Blondie, I'm so sorry. I really...."

"Just shut up! Shut up! Do you realise what you have done? Do you realise how you have fucked up my entire fucking life? I can't even talk to you like this." As if she caught herself. "You're only a child Izzie, a child. I have been sleeping with a fucking child."

As though she had realised only for the first time, tears flowed down her cheeks. She was blood red and I didn't know what to say or do. Seeing her in pain only caused me pain and I couldn't respond. I just cried.

"Don't you have anything to say? Are you just going to sit there and say nothing? Say something! Anything! But say something. Tell me it's a lie and that this is just a fucking prank!" She cried harder.

I went over to hold her as she fell to the ground. She fought me off at first, then she allowed me to hold her and just cried. I couldn't take back what I had done, I just cried with her. It just happened naturally.

"Izzie!!! Why did you do this? I'm going to lose everything!!" she screamed.

"I'm sorry, I'm so sorry." I didn't know what else to say.

We barely spoke. She wanted to turn herself into the police, but I begged her not to and told her that she'd never see me again. She never did.

* * * * *

In my letter, I apologised to her. Told her how I fell in love with her and wanted her love. I found her on Facebook and I sent her my letter. For weeks she didn't respond then finally she messaged back. She told me she'd forgiven me and asked about my life. She was married now, to a man and they had three children together. I suppose I can conclude that I definitely ruined something inside her, because according to her, I was the last girl she dated.

# Girlfriend No.5

This is where the downward spiral in my life really began. It started with the Malaysian I moved across the world for. Our encounter originally started out as an affair. I was living with my then girlfriend, Nigerian born, Omi. I believed I loved her, because, even after walking in on her engaged in a threesome with two men she had introduced to me as her cousins, I still stuck around broken-hearted and all. My only remedy was to divert my attention elsewhere, seek some form of love and affection now and then from other women. I knew I should have left Omi, but she had a way of just bending me to her will and no matter what she'd done, I'd soon forgiven her or rather pushed it to the back of my mind and moved on. She wasn't particularly drop dead gorgeous, but she possessed the type of beauty that just captivated me. Her skin was like velvet, the type of dark that was just cool and enchanting and I lived for it. Added to that, she was a homemaker and provided much of which I wasn't quite familiar with but needed.

In the midst of our madness, I bumped into a Malaysian beauty almost twice my age. I was besotted with her, something about her pulled me in and kept pulling me in. Then in the blink of an eye, there was a U-Haul outside mine and Omi's apartment while she was at work and soon I was gone. My love affair had turned into a full-blown relationship. I didn't even have the courtesy to leave Omi a note or properly end it with her. However, after thinking about everything that she had put me through, all the nights I had stayed up crying wishing I could just escape her once and for all, I figured leaving her stuck with the full month's rent was payback enough. She didn't really deserve my time, let alone an apology.

* * * * *

I was only eighteen when I moved for her and our reason for moving was that she'd overstayed her visa in the US and was being deported back to Malaysia. I thought I was madly in love with her, so instead of staying in the US and finding another girlfriend to ruin, I decided to move out there to be with her. At the time, I thought she was amazing; she was a nature lover who would have probably been a brain surgeon if not for the fact that she had Attention Deficit Disorder. Not that people with ADD can't become brain surgeons, it's just that she allowed it to get in her way. She refused to accept that sometimes we just have to follow rather than lead or the need to just settle down and get things done. She also didn't want to accept that she had a problem, so even after filling her prescriptions, she'd never take the medication. As a result, she'd only acquired a high school diploma.

We dated in America for almost six months. I knew early in the relationship that it wouldn't work, but I tried nonetheless. She was what I'd call too much for me. On the plus side, she was very smart and ambitious but the downside of that was she had a jealous streak. It's not what you think though. She was very pompous, so she didn't imagine anyone could cheat on her. Her jealousy was directed towards the person she was with. I completed all my college courses before I turned sixteen and was working on a bachelor's degree. I was apparently advanced which my Math teacher had noticed and had made it her task to guide me through acquiring advanced education. She was not very happy that I was leaving the country months before completing my degree, but I planned to complete my courses and travel back to write my final exams, which seemed to have brought her some peace. For my dear girlfriend Nurin, though she claimed to admire this and would tell all her friends about my accomplishments, it all somehow seemed to affect her ego.

I got a job in a restaurant in Kuala Lumpur as a waitress. Nurin was struggling to hold down a job. Only two months being back, she had lost seven jobs and was on her eighth one. I decided to ask my manager to give her a job and I could tell the poor sod didn't have the capacity to take her on but did anyway because he had a soft spot for me. I didn't even sort my work permit and he knew this, but he paid me under the table and kept me

on. Then came Nurin like a fucking world wind.
Malaysia wasn't the place to let people know that
we were in a romantic relationship. If I had
known how it was before moving there, I would
have probably had a bit of rethink; but I was there
and there was no going back. I learned not to
touch her on the street and stealing a kiss in
public was out of the question. Her family knew
though, and they were pretty accepting of our
relationship. Her sister was a wealthy business
owner in Malaysia and also a lesbian, which
everyone knew but I suppose that because of her
wealth, no one really bothered her or the family.
She never got along with Nurin and Nurin hated
the fact that I got along well with her.

Only two weeks in, Nurin got into a huge
argument with my manager. Apparently, she
didn't see why he should be upset with the fact

that she turned up late for work and wasn't in uniform. Instead of apologising, trying to make it right she kicked off and you might have guessed dragged me right into it with her. He fired her on the spot and while I was picking up the dishes from a table I was waiting on, she dragged me so hard, the plates and glasses shattered on the tiled floor and we were gone.

I was infuriated! I had struggled to get the job, because I didn't have the legal right to work in the country; she had demanded that I not accept the job that was being offered to me by her sister; had been incapable of holding a job down and now this! We needed to eat! We needed an income and for some reason, she just couldn't get in.

Arriving at the family home we stayed in with her parents, I retired to our room, buried my head in the pillow and screamed. I wanted to get away from her. I wasn't making time to study and now everything was falling apart, because she just couldn't comprehend that one cannot always lead; and in her fucked up world, if she wasn't steering the vehicle, then the vehicle just wasn't moving.

* * * * *

I'd been living in Malaysia for almost three months. After much arguing and lecturing from her mother, she finally allowed me to take a job at one of her sister's company. By this time, I had had enough of Nurin and wanted out of Malaysia and back to my life in New York. I needed some peace and stability and were it not for the atmosphere being so conservative, I'm sure I would have found someone to mess around with.

Then came trouble. I noticed it brewing and I tried to ignore it. I knew that it wasn't just a matter of taking an interest in me, Puteri fancied me.

Her main office was in another building where her managers sat and where the operations of her business were headed, but she kept stopping in almost every day to "check in on me". Each time she came by - which was literally every day, she'd bring me something else.

One afternoon, the Monday after my nineteenth birthday, she showed up with a gift bag. I found it strange because she'd been over for lunch the day before and had already gifted me an H&M voucher. She sat on my desk while I unboxed the Rolex watch she had bought me.

"I can't accept this. Is this even real? Why would you buy me such a gift?"

"What do you mean?"

"I mean, this isn't cheap. This is a Rolex watch!"

"I meant, what do you mean if it's real."

"I don't know. Like is it a knockoff from Thailand?"

She laughed, "I didn't even know that they sold knockoffs in Thailand? But to answer your question, yes, it is real and I wanted you to have it because you deserve it."

"Wait, this is a trick right. You and Nurin have planned this. You're trying to mess me around, aren't you?"

"No no no no, Nu doesn't know, and I don't want her to know. There's enough tension between us. One less thing to fight about would be good."

"But I can't accept this. It's just not appropriate, I mean, what will your girlfriend think?"

"I don't have a girlfriend anymore, so nothing to worry about there."

"Hmmm, I really can't though and just as you don't want to fight with Nurin, I don't either and this will just be another thing for her to bite my head off about. Thanks for the thought but I really can't accept this. Plus, I wouldn't know where to say I got it."

"Tell her it's a fake from Thailand." She laughs

'Oh, come on," I smiled, I could feel myself blushing, "she'd never believe that".  I tried to hand her back the bag that I had tucked the watch back into neatly.

"Sorry, have to go. Have a meeting in like five minutes." She walked away leaving my hand outstretched, the bag still dangling from it. "See you later Izzie." She winked at me as she always did each time she left.

The problem I had was that I was attracted to Puteri. She took an interest in me that Nurin didn't. We had long conversations and she'd always want to know about my dreams, always looking into things to see how she could help me achieve one thing or another. She was busy getting me a work permit which she had paid for herself entirely. She had arranged for me to be able to study while at work or do my assignments because I couldn't get a break from Nurin at home to do anything but attend to her needs and was always coming up with one solution or another to my problems. Next to my Math teacher, she was the only other person who really seemed to care about my future.

* * * * *

The time came for me to fly back to the US to take my final exams and complete my degree. My plan was to go back and not return to be with Nurin. I planned not to tell her. She couldn't enter the US so there was no way for her to come after me. In my mind it was my perfect get away plan and boy did I want to get away from her. Life with her had become draining and stagnant. It wasn't the life I wanted for myself and I was going to get away from it at whatever cost. So, with my exams coming up it was the perfect getaway.

"What are you doing now?" she questioned entering the bedroom.

"Aw, good you've come home, I need a bit of help finding a ticket."

"A ticket to where, where are we going?"

"Have you forgotten that I have final exams coming up soon?"

"Which exams, I thought you were finished with school?"

"Why are you messing around? Be serious, the tickets keep going up, so I need to buy one asap. Can you help me find one please?"

"If, I must." She reached for her laptop begrudgingly. "What dates are you looking for?"

"Well, I need to be back a week before my exams start so I'd say around May 14$^{th}$ or thereabouts."

"Woa, wait a minute, when do you plan to come back?"

"I'm not sure yet. I need to wait for everything to be finalised, plus spend some time with my mom once exams are through."

"Spend time with your mom? What for?"

"What do you mean, I haven't seen her in months. I need to....."

"Why do you need to see her? You need to go sit your exams and come right back!"

"Are you crazy Nurin? Why would I go home and not spend time with my mother?"

"Why are you so interested in spending time with your mother all of a sudden, what are you planning to do? You don't even go to see your mother when you live in New York. Do you think I'm stupid?"

I should have known I'd have needed a better excuse. She was right, the sudden interest in my mother was just not a good excuse. I shot myself in the foot there and just like that, another argument started between us.

"You know what your problem is Izzie, you think too god damn much of yourself. Always thinking you're smarter than everyone else. Why the hell do you need to go sit some stupid exam anyway? What is that degree going to do for you? You have a good job, one that pays. This constant wanting this and that is getting on my last nerve. You should be focused on making a home here. You should stop working as well, be a real woman. I should come home to dinner, washed clothes and all the things a good woman provides. As a matter of fact, I'm putting this laptop down. Get off the bed with all that rubbish so I can lie down."

I could feel myself wanting to respond but thought it better to restrain myself, so the argument doesn't blow up.

"You think too much of yourself. Imagine if you were beautiful? Always walking around looking down on everyone as if you're some sort of gift to mankind. You irritate the shit out of me. Even my mother doesn't like you because of your god damn ways and behaviour." She wasn't going to stop.

"We don't have to talk about me and my exams and you have decided not to help, so can we please just let it go?"

"Who the hell do you think you're talking to? Do I look like your house girl? Don't you dare act as if you are better than me, because you're not. Your problem is that you're young and foolish. You never take my advice, always thinking you know best. Miss Know It All."

I began to walk out of the room, then she threw the pillow at me. I picked it up, placed it at the foot of the bed and turned towards the door. Again, the pillow was thrown at me but this time, I decided to leave it on the floor and leave the room anyway. This was a pattern with her. Everything I did offended her, and she was always quick to give me a proper telling off.

* * * * *

The following day at work, Puteri came to visit but in the morning. Like many other times, her mother had called her to tell her of the way "I was being mistreated by Nurin". Problem is, her mother never called her into order. Other than Puteri, everyone seemed afraid of her. I wasn't afraid, I just genuinely couldn't be bothered.

Before leaving, Puteri booked a ticket which was sent to my email, paid in full by her. I was grateful yet uncomfortable for her spending on me and paying me attention. I kept the watch she had gifted me in my drawer at work along with a pair of earrings I had found on my desk and knew she had left it there. The problem is the card with the earrings had read "your secret admirer". They were obviously diamonds, so I knew they must have been from her. We never spoke of them though.

* * * * *

May 10<sup>th</sup> came it was going to be my last day at work and Puteri had organised for all the staff members to come to a lunch she had arranged at a five-star restaurant I had been dying to visit but never had the chance to. She knew that I wanted to go there, because it had come up in one of our many conversations.

After lunch, she drove me back to the office. Upon leaving her car, she rested her hand on my thigh, so close to my vagina that it sent shivers through my entire body. When our eyes met she leaned in to kiss me and I pulled her closer to me and kissed her back. I felt myself pushing my body closer to hers and restrained myself. I grabbed hold of myself and pulled away from her opened the car door and exited in a rush. My heart was racing. I couldn't take back what had happened and a part of me didn't want to either. I was shaking. I didn't want to go back to my desk in the state that I was in, so I went into the bathroom on the ground floor adjacent to the main reception.

Upon returning to my desk, Puteri was perched on my chair swivelling slowly from left to right, right to left again and again, her head thrown back towards the ceiling, her eyes closed. In that moment. I wanted to kiss her some more, but every bit of me knew it was wrong. I turned to walk away and she grabbed my arm.

"Hey, where are you going?"

"Please don't do that, everyone is watching." I attempted to whisper.

"Can we talk? Let's go for a walk."

I didn't want to go for a walk with her, I didn't want to have the opportunity to act on anything that I was feeling. But I could feel everyone's eyes on me and I didn't want to make it more awkward.

"Yeah, why not," I smirked.

We walked down the street a few blocks, me on the inside, her shielding me from the possibility of biker thieves riding up next to me and robbing me of whatever they'd see fit. For a while we said nothing. We just walked. I sensed that she didn't know what to say and was worried that I might be angry with her, but I wasn't angry. I should have been, but I wasn't. Bad as it seemed, I had longed for some form of sexual attention and I wasn't getting any from Nurin. We argued every day and I just couldn't be turned on by her. At nights while she slept, if I had the urge I'd masturbate, but lesbian deathbed had reached us months ago.

As if to shield her from her thoughts I finally said, "It's crazy, I shouldn't like that, and neither should you because I'm with your sister. But I liked it, and I hope you liked it too."

A sense of relief appeared on her face, "I thought you wanted to kill me and yes, I know I probably shouldn't feel the way I do, but I do and that's reality. I fell in love with you the moment I laid eyes on you. I want to be with you."

"But..."

"Please don't reject me Izzie, can we at least try. If it doesn't work out, I promise, I'll walk away but can we try?"

"But what about Nurin, what will she think? What will your parents think?"

"We don't have to stay here, we can go anywhere you want to go, tonight if you wish."

"Oh Puteri, I can't think. This is too much."

She walked over and hugged me. I squeezed her. She was homely, for the first time in a long time I felt safe. I felt wanted and loved. Though I didn't know if she loved me, I felt loved and I wanted to stay there in her arms.

"We can't do this. Your mother already hates me."

"What, where did you get that, my mother loves you. She adores you."

"No, she doesn't." I began to sob as all the fights
I had had with Nurin, all the hateful things she'd
said came flooding in my mind and I just wanted
to go back to New York and forget about the
months I had had with her.

"Hey, come on. Don't cry, please. What shall I
do?"

"I don't know," I sobbed even more at the
thought that she was being so caring.

"Izzie, everything is okay. I promise you it is. We
don't have to make any decisions now. I'm
sorry."

"What are you sorry for?"

"For upsetting you, causing you to hurt."

"But you haven't. I, I, I...."

"You what?"

"I want to be with you too, but I don't think we can, it's not right."

She pulled me closer to her bosom, wrapped her arms around me tighter and I inhaled her scent as I found comfort in her arms.

* * * * *

I wrote Nurin a letter and decided to send it on email.

I had long apologised, but she never accepted my apology, understandably. Nonetheless, I owed her an explanation, so I wrote it all down and hit send from my yahoo account. As though she was sat by her computer waiting to hear from me, she responded before I finished typing up my next letter of apology.

Her response included the fact that she wanted to reach out to me, but thought I'd never respond to her.

I invited her to messenger and we spent hours talking and you would not have guessed, without knowing I was having an online affair with a woman I knew for a fact I didn't want a relationship with. Within days of talking to her, I realised she hadn't really changed. However, as if I was trying to make up for what I had done to her, I kept on chatting with her about everything and nothing. She was in a relationship with a girl she claimed not to love.

A few days in, a few sex chats later I decided to tell Nurin that this wasn't what I wanted. I decided to come clean before it got any further and I'm sure you might have guessed it; Nurin, keeping true to her nature gave me a proper telling off when I told her I didn't want to pursue our "relationship" any further. A tad bit hurtful it was reading the first few lines, but I was pleased with myself that I had dodged the bullet yet again. I had escaped the grips of Nurin once and for all. I had nothing to be guilty of, so we could both move on with our lives.

# Fiancé No.1

Puteri and I left Malaysia on the flight to New York on May 13th. She'd bought two tickets and had planned to surprise me, and I was happy she did, after the unveiling of "Us".

She dropped me home the last day of work and for some reason, Nurin came out to the car and found her hand resting on my thigh. She came up to the car while we were engaged in conversation with each other gazing into each other's eyes, hence, neither of us had seen her. True to form, Nurin had no issues with causing a scene no matter who was watching. So, she dragged me out of the car and started at Puteri who raced out of the car to my rescue. Her mother had come to the gateway to investigate the chaos and had found us three in nothing short of a brawl; Nurin the main attraction, at the top of her voice making all kinds of threats.

In the end, Puteri and her mother gathered my things and I was taken back to her place where I stayed until our departure. Yes, Nurin turned up there as well and unleashed her wrath.

* * * * *

After my exams ended, Puteri, my PuBear, took me to Thailand where we had decided we'd settle; to look for an apartment. She needed to stay in Malaysia for work but have me close enough, so she could fly home for the weekends and Bangkok was both liberal and close for us to have the life we wanted. I think she was the first woman that I had genuinely felt for after Pricilla. Puteri provided much to my emotional needs and provided the support I needed to be able to dream, plus set and achieve my goals. We had a great connection and it was quite a difference to hear friends say they could tell how much she loved me based on the way she looked at me.

Our lives involved working; her in Malaysia and me in Thailand where I had secured a job as an ESOL teacher. I was already reading for my masters and was hoping that I'd be able to get into a distance learning program; both Puteri and I were already on the lookout for something. On Friday mornings, sometimes Thursday evenings, Puteri would be home for a long weekend. We both liked cooking and spent a lot of time taking cooking classes or cooking up some kind of storm from a cookbook we had picked out somewhere.

At Christmas, she came home for three long weeks and it was bliss. Her mother came to visit, and it wasn't as dreadful as I had imagined it being. She showed more interest in me and wanted to know about me. I had believed every single time Nurin said she didn't like me, because after days of moving in and the first huge argument between me and Nurin, she seemed to have genuinely lost interest and never made or entertained many conversations with me. It was often like pulling teeth, so after a few tries, I'd retreated into myself and left her alone. But when she visited, she was the total opposite; affectionate and talkative all at the same time. It was nice for the three of us to engage in activities; she even showed me how to cook hae mee, roti canai and all the components of nasi lemak, which were some of Puteri's favourite dishes. Everything was perfect.

* * * * *

The following May came and Puteri flew us to Sydney to celebrate our anniversary. On the final day of our five days' vacation, she took me out to a beautiful seafood restaurant on Bondi Beach. At first, I thought the restaurant was closed, because there was no one there when we entered except for staff members who all seemed over attentive. It was obvious that they had gone out of their way to decorate the venue, as there were thousands of red roses adorning the entire room. To my surprise, we were led to a table over-looking the beach and for some reason the two waitresses couldn't stop smiling; it was evident they knew more than I did.

"What's going on darling?" I questioned quietly.

She smiled in response, "I'm treating my lady to dinner, anything wrong with that?"

"Well nothing is wrong, but we are the only ones here. You didn't need to do this."

"Well of course I needed to. It's our anniversary. You've put up with all of me for the past year and I wanted to thank you."

"Come on PuBear, you don't need to thank me. I love you. You're the one who puts up with me and all my moods."

She reached out to cup my face, "Izzie, you're the best thing that's ever happened to me. You've given me the will to dream and to be myself. Every day of my life is more exciting than the other and that's because I get to wake up to you whether on the phone or in our bed. You are my entire world Izzie, I can't imagine my life without you."

I could feel the tears welling up in the back of my throat and worried that if I began to speak I'd cry. I didn't want the waitresses to see my tears and think that I was sad, because at that moment I was the happiest girl in Sydney and possibly even the world. "Oh PuBear," I struggled to get the words out, "you are my everything, you are my world, I can't imagine my world without you for a minute." A tear fell from my eye.

"Oh Izzie," she dried my eyes, "please don't cry. We'll always be together; until my last breath. I'll make sure of it, if it's the last thing I do." She squeezed both my cheeks. "Come on, think happy thoughts and let's observe the beauty beneath us."

"I'd rather observe the beauty sitting next to me," I joked.

We ate the most amazing food and engaged in conversation with each other, while the two waitresses remained attentive. When our main meal arrived, it was carried by the chef himself. It almost floored me, because I had tried so many recipes from so many of his books. I was obsessed with the young Three Star Michellin chef. I was speechless. For a moment I forgot that Puteri was next to me and became wrapped up in conversation with him, when finally he said he'd leave us to our meal and retired to the kitchen. She had pulled out all the stops, had gone all out to make it a super extra special day for us. I was over the moon.

"You are full of surprises!"

She smiled at me, "Well, my lady likes surprises and I provide what my lady likes."

I couldn't imagine how I'd thank her for everything. "You're amazing, absolutely amazing."

"I know," she smiled.

"Yes you are. You really are."

We finally ate, and every bite I took was more special knowing that I was eating his food. Puteri pointed out the fact that I wasn't as talkative through the main, a state I'd usually find myself in when I became taken over by food. I was an enthusiastic foodie and I loved cooking, but liked eating even more. My second glass of champagne arrived with dessert and I didn't pay attention to it. I dived into the apple sorbet filled sugar apple which tasted of pure crisp heaven. A fork fell to the floor, but neither of the waitresses rushed to its rescue as they had done to save the napkin that I had dropped earlier at dinner or the fork that I had brushed off the table while belting a belly laugh to one of Puteri's jokes. It was Puteri who bent to pick up the fork this time, but she didn't just get up, she took a moment too long then I observed her on one knee, hand outstretched awaiting my attention.

"Isabel Anne Sanders, I do not want to spend a day of my life without you. I want to be with you and only you until my last breath. Will you do me the honour of being my wife?"

Tears were already flowing down my cheeks and I must have paused for a moment too long, because I could see despair on her face, "Yes, I'll be your Mrs. Megat." Without thinking, I reached down and kissed her. She must have also forgotten where we were, because she kissed me back. There was suddenly applause around us. When my eyes finally opened, the entire staff were standing there and I could see one of the waitresses who had been tending to us sobbing.

The other walked over to our table and handed me my champagne. "Don't drink it too fast," She instructed. As soon as my eyes caught the glass, I could see the emerald cut diamond ring at the bottom of the glass.

"Oh my god! Yes." I screamed as if she had not already proposed. I turn to pour the champagne into my water glass that was sitting on the table. Puteri took the glass from me and recovered the ring placing it delicately on my finger. "Yes, yes, yes, yes, yes a thousand times!" I yelled.

The small crowd watching us laughed in unison.

"You already said yes my love," she giggled.

* * * * *

Everything was going well for us. I was planning our "wedding" and Puteri remained as perfect as she had been. It must have been too perfect in my mind because for whatever reason I decided to go and mess it all up.

She had been away on business for almost two weeks trying to sign a new contract. She called every chance she got, but for some reason, it wasn't enough. I needed some form of distraction, so I called up the few girlfriends I had in Bangkok to come over for a drink at the apartment. I made drinks and ordered in food for all six of us.

When they came over, we talked and talked, and I opened up about the frustration of Puteri being away for so long. It was a relief to talk to someone about it; with someone other than her. The girls were understanding and supportive.

I hadn't realised before, but my Canadian friend Krystal who had been sitting next to me on the sofa, consoling me by touching my back all too sensual; seemed to have taken quite an interest in me. Everyone was either picked up by a driver or headed to the parking garage to drive home, but Krystal lingered after everyone left and seemed not to have any interest in leaving. She got up and went to the kitchen, returning with two glasses for us. By that time I had already had three glasses of wine, so I refused the glass and walked to the kitchen to make a cup of jasmine tea.

"Izzie, I checked but couldn't see any. Do you by chance have a Singha beer?" She walked into the kitchen leaning over the island.

"Yeah," I reached for one in the wine fridge beneath the counter, opened it and handed it to her.

"May I ask, what do you plan on doing with this Puteri thing?"

"What do you mean?"

"Like the fact that you guys are having problems, are you still going to go ahead with the wedding?"

"This is temporary Krys, as soon as she gets the chance she will come home. She's a businesswoman so it's expected that she'll not always be around. I just have to accept that. It's just been particularly hard this time around as it's the longest we've been apart."

"But do you think you'd be able to do that for the rest of your life? What happens when you have a child?"

"Come on Krys, let's not talk about this anymore, it's upsetting as it is."

"Okay sorry, we don't have to talk about it anymore. I'm sorry."

I suddenly had the urge to wash the dishes. I decided against putting them in the dishwasher. I found water therapeutic and wanted a moment of escape. In my opinion, I was possibly blowing it out of proportion because it was only two weeks since I last saw her. Nonetheless, I was spoilt. We spent three sometimes four days out of the week together. My body was used to having her home. I found myself drifting into my thoughts and suddenly my shoulders were being massaged.

"Hey, relax. You're tensed."

"I'm okay," I didn't feel uncomfortable until she reached her hand under my arms and started caressing my breast and kissing my neck.

Comfort turned to relief then to wanting and I turned to kiss her. We had sex in the kitchen, then made our way to the bedroom. It was as though I had been completely deprived of the human touch for decades. We had sex over and over and over again.

The following morning, I woke up with pure guilt when I opened my eyes to find Krystal lying in Puteri's place.

I never saw Krystal again. I left her calls unanswered and unreturned.

* * * * *

I couldn't get rid of the guilt of cheating on my PuBear, who I had promised monogamy. She began to notice that something was wrong and the fact that I was no longer engulfed in the planning of our wedding worried her. She kept asking probing questions trying to figure out what was wrong and why I had become reserved or constantly wandered off with my thoughts sometimes in the middle of our conversations. I couldn't dare tell her. I couldn't confess it.

The business deal meant that she was gone for weeks at a time. She begged for my patience and promised she'd take time off to spend with me once things settled down. I was looking forward to it, but the guilt that filled me kept driving a wedge between us and not getting a response to my messages within seconds, as it had been in the past, began to get to me. She was the one I spoke to the most. Walking down the street, I'd see something funny and message her immediately about it. Whatever the case or whatever was happening, I would want to talk to my PuBear about it first.

I got accepted into a Master's programme at the University of South Australia. The email came in while I was having breakfast on the sofa. I wanted to tell her first, so I reached for my phone and rang her but there was no answer. On the second attempt, my call was rejected.

I waited a few minutes but there was no message or call back, so to distract myself I reached for my laptop and logged on to Facebook. I checked my messages to see whether there were any new messages. I didn't care much for Facebook; I rarely posted anything and would only log on once per week, if that much to check messages and respond to them. Now and again I would catch someone online, especially my friends back in America and decide to chat for long periods. Scrolling through my messages, I realised I had missed or skipped a few. One of them was from a

girl who's account name was "Queen Dyke". I
suppose I had ignored it before because I found
it too cliched and immature to have such an
account name. Against my better judgement, I
decided to open the message and read what she
had said.

There were tons of messages from her at different
times. The last one noted my refusal to respond
to her and advised that she'd gotten the message
and wouldn't message again. I decided to respond
to her and started off by apologising for not
responding to her long list of messages. It said
she was online, but I was a bit wary of sending the
message and having to carry on a pointless
conversation but sent it anyway. It wouldn't do
much harm and I wanted the distraction.

Queen Dyke was actually a 23 years old Biology
student in Dusseldorf named Vusiwana. She

wasn't as shallow as I imagined she'd be. We chatted for hours until I finally got a call from Puteri who was in a meeting and couldn't have taken my call. I wasn't pleased as it had been more than four hours before she responded to me. I decided not to tell her about my news. She seemed distracted and for the first time, I wondered whether she was having an affair or if she was really away on work. I couldn't feel anything in my gut that told me she wasn't being faithful, but my mind got the better of me.

* * * * *

Vusi provided what Puteri had stopped providing; she gave me attention. The weeks she was away, began to be more bearable and I looked forward to chatting with Vusi. I restricted myself from calling her, deleted my messages with her and tried to erase any evidence of her when Puteri was home. I found myself wanting the constant attention I was getting from Vusi.

She came home late on Saturday, but said she had to leave again early Monday morning. It didn't move me, I was used to her shorter stays now and didn't really get bothered by the fact that she was there. That weekend we didn't cook or anything. I could sense that she was trying hard to make up for being away and having to do her job, but I couldn't bear it anymore and it was showing. The promise of her being away and fully immersed in this new business deal coming to an end soon fell on deaf ears.

When she left on Monday morning I was still in bed and the sun was nowhere near being up. I could hear her talking to the driver when she put him on hold to kiss me goodbye.

"Please be patient with me my love. It will all end soon and I will make it all up to you. I promise you I will." She touched my face and I could feel her trembling.

Sitting up in bed, I took her hand, "hey, what's wrong? You're shaking."

"I'm fucking up the one thing that means the most to me Izzie, and it scares me. It's affecting my work as well."

"What do you mean?"

"I feel as though I'm not enough for you, as though we won't make it."

I scanned the room to see if she'd by chance been on my computer and seen messages from Vusi. The computer wasn't in the bedroom which was a relief. "Come on PuBear, you said this will be over soon right. I'll be here when it's over." I kissed her forehead and she nestled into my bosom. I felt I was lying to myself, but knew that I didn't want to see her hurt.

"I couldn't bear it Izzie. I couldn't bear losing your love."

* * * * *

It had been eight days since she left for Kuala Lumpur and three days since I heard from her. I was riddled with worry and her mother had not heard from her either. I got hold of her PA who said she'd been busy, and she'd pass my message on. She kept telling me that for three entire days. When Puteri finally called, we had our first ever huge argument. It was more than the occasional disagreements we had. I was screaming. I couldn't understand why she never called or messaged for three whole fucking days. She had time to sleep, so why didn't she call me before bed? She was full of excuses and none of them were acceptable. I hung up the phone in the middle of her apologising.

The day after, I fell in the shower so hard my back ached and ached. Puteri didn't call when I messaged her asking to call me immediately. Our driver took me to the hospital and my friend Elle met me there. She called Puteri a few times but there was no answer or response. Eventually, I asked her to stop calling and when I got home, it was Vusi who kept me company. Puteri finally called later in the night, but I didn't tell her what had happened. She hung up and rang back to ask why I hadn't told her; she'd rang Elle who told her the entire story. She promised she'd be home the following day and all of a sudden I felt guilty for being an asshole.

The next day came and went and so did the next.
I couldn't go to work. By the third day, the pain
was significantly less and I could walk about
without much constraints. She was still not home.
Night came, and I was sat in bed after 12am with
a glass of wine and tears running down my cheeks
wondering why I wasn't important enough for her
to come home. I wrote a simple note, took my
ring off, laid it on the note next to the bed and
booked a flight to Dusseldorf. I moved to a hotel
the following day, switched my phone off and the
day after, I got into the taxi arranged by the hotel
for me and made my way to the airport.

* * * * *

I'm saving this letter for last as it was the hardest
for me to write.

# Affair No.7

Vusi and I were dating when I got into a relationship with Lorelei. Thing is, Vusi and I just wouldn't have worked out. At almost 21, I was set on achieving my goals and nights out drinking until dawn wasn't really something I found particularly interesting. Drunkenness did not intrigue me, nor did women who got frisky with everyone and anyone after a few drinks. She was also controlling and irritated the life out of me when I'd put something on and she'd attempt to demand that I take it off. Her hand was also light. After a few weeks of living with her, I decided to invest the bit of money I had saved up into getting an apartment for myself.

Soon, I got into university to study full time. I was accepted for a second Masters and was going to have to invest a lot of time and effort into acquiring them both simultaneously. For some reason, I couldn't shake Vusi, because we'd break up then she'd show up drunk at my apartment literally falling on her face and I'd let her in to sleep it off. Then weeks later, she'd drive me over the wall again and I'd break it off once more. She was not the type of woman who liked dating and she was much like Nurin: she had a particularly short fuse. A genius she was, but a godforsaken angry one. Everything irritated her; sometimes even my darn breathing.

At school, I met the very shy unassuming Lorelei. She was a pretty girl, but again not my type and for more reasons than one. She was an extreme introvert who also became frisky after a few drinks, wasn't much for conversations and was awfully ditzy. Sometimes, the rare moments when she actually tried to engage in conversations, one would be baffled that she'd actually made it into university let alone into a computer science Master's program. I always thought though that it was her good-natured ways that kept me interested. She wasn't good-natured and kind-hearted towards other people; just me. She was known for being antisocial and pretty rude by most. When we finally created a friend group which she was a part of, most people wouldn't want to hang out if she was going to be there. She could be pretty draining and quite the downer; never really had much good to say about anyone or anything. She could easily make the devil out of a newborn baby in just one sentence. She was very weird, but good in bed and that was where most of our interaction happened. I knew too that we would never be long-term partners or at all. I made it a point to never entertain the idea that we were in a relationship because I really didn't want one with her but she served her purpose. Vusi saw me with her a few times too many and concluded that we were in a relationship and eventually stopped showing up to my door half drunk in the middle of the night. She soon blocked me on Facebook and it was a relief.

Lorelei became my constant, she spent a lot of time with me at my apartment and a lot of people assumed we were an item, an assumption I would always refute when she wasn't present or otherwise smile in response when she was standing next to me or close enough. She was clingy too, which was a major turn off for me. In the midst of whatever it was that we were doing, I had two major affairs with two women who were close friends, and each thought they were my only.

Olivia and Elsa had been close friends for most of their lives. They grew up next door to each other when Elsa and her parents moved here from Sweden when she was only ten years old. They had a close bond, but neither knew that the other was interested in women.  Elsa was a "good Catholic girl" and I genuinely cared for her. She was the only virgin amongst us. She was saving herself for marriage based on what she told us and at 24, no one had ever seen her with a boy or man, so we all believed and supported her in terms of her choice. I met Elsa through Olivia and we quickly became friends. It was one of those things where you met someone and within a split second, you knew you'd be good, if not great friends. As we got closer, I became more and more protective of her. She was pure, I'd often tell myself: an uncorrupted being who loved everyone and was loved by everyone around her.

It wasn't long that she'd be part of the gang in our slumber parties. Only Olivia had a child who she shared custody of with her ex-husband; so it was easy to organise overnight hangouts whether at someone's apartment or in some sort of accommodation in another city for a weekend getaway.

The good thing was that I was completely distracted from what I was really feeling inside. There were times when I'd sit and daydream about Puteri, about what she was doing, how she was; whether she'd eaten or slept, whether she was happy; everything. I wanted to know that wherever she was, she was being loved. She was a good person who deserved to have someone there to come home to. I loved her and often thought of racing to find her, but would remember the nights I laid in bed crying because

I didn't hear from her. I didn't want that for myself. Yes, I didn't quite know what I wanted in a relationship, but I knew I didn't want that.

In response, my self-destructive nature kicked in, basically taking centre stage and I headed on a downward spiral.

* * * * *

Without even trying, I was sleeping with Olivia, Lorelei and Elsa all at the same time. Whatever it was with Elsa, it really took control of me.

It started as a mere exchange of texts messages. She'd message me in the middle of the afternoon to see what I was doing and if I wasn't studying or working at the plant, I'd always take up her offer of going out for coffee in the middle of the day to one of the many cafés across town. I noticed that we were getting closer when she started messaging me first thing in the mornings. Lorelei quickly began to express her dislike of Elsa and warned that she had a crush on me, but I never paid that idea much thought with it coming from Lorelei. She thought everyone had a crush on me and had a problem with every single friend I took interest in, male or female. She hated my god damn cat for god's sakes; according to her the cat needed too much of my attention and whenever she'd come near me when Lorelei was around, she'd be shooed away.

I genuinely didn't like Lorelei much, but for some reason, I kept her around. Well as I said, she was good in bed. She knew how to get me to an orgasm at the right speed and the gentleness that came with it blew my mind. The other good thing was that she liked being pounded with a strap-on and I soon realised that I liked that fact;

the bigger the strap on got, the more she opened up. It was exciting. Not being connected to her made it easier to have wild sex with her. I knew for a fact it was nothing more than that, based on the fact that I couldn't kiss her.

So back to Elsa; she kept messaging me in the mornings, then one evening she turned up at my door uninvited with an overnight bag.

"Hey, what's up?" I reached out in the doorway to hug her.

She walked into the hallway, placing her bag on the floor. I was wearing a pair of yoga shorts and a sports bra. I'd just finished my 5k run on the treadmill and was having a cup of jasmine tea. She came in and sat on the single chair next to the Orchids Table. I called it my orchid table because I had made the mistake of telling my friends I liked orchid and six people had turned up at my housewarming; orchid in hand. So, I ended up with more than needed and had to dedicate an entire table to four of them.

"So where are you off to then?"

"Here."

"Oh, okay. Are you sleeping over?"

"If you don't mind."

"Why didn't you tell me when we met up this afternoon?"

"I didn't want any objections."

I laughed, "objections, what do you mean?"

"Because I asked twice already, and you made excuses. So, I decided to take matters into my own hands and invite myself over."

"Well that's one way of doing it isn't it."

While in the shower, Elsa came in and plastered herself on the bowl while she watched me shower. For some reason, I wasn't particularly comfortable with the way she watched me and when she offered to give me a hand, I quickly objected. I truly didn't want to be the source of her corruption. I wanted her to find true love and marry the man of her dreams; therefore, I pushed away any thought I had or any advances she made. I wasn't in a place for relationships either, my broken heart wasn't healed, and I wasn't going to be rushing into settling down any time soon. I liked the freedom I had. I could go out on the town with the girls, meet a girl in the club, take her to the bathroom and finger fuck her in one of the stalls and feel no sense of guilt whatsoever. I could go home after all my antics and sleep well not having to worry about anyone's feelings. I didn't want my life to change anytime soon and Elsa wasn't the type of girl I wanted to mess with.

In the middle of the night, I felt my back being kissed and fingernails trailing down my thigh. Initially, I was confused but soon realised that Elsa was making advances. I rolled over and she ran her hand down my belly, trailed over my belly button, then over my vagina and between my thighs. I moaned when she suddenly squeezed my pussy. She wasted no time, within a second, she was between my thighs and her head was buried in my pussy. She was better than Lorelei was; far better. She sucked me, her tongue flickered over my clitoris, then penetrated me repeatedly bringing me to orgasm. When she was finished, she came up to kiss me and for some reason, I couldn't. Since Puteri, I found it hard to kiss anyone. Moments in, I'd think of her and retract. I held her as she laid on top of me. I was conscious of the fact that I didn't want to touch her and that I didn't want to corrupt her, so I didn't.

That was the beginning of our supposed affair. The months that followed carried on pretty much the same as far as sex was concerned. She'd go down on me and I'd refuse to touch her. She kept asking for reciprocity and a commitment, but I often reminded her of her not wanting to disappoint her parents and she'd take heed and leave the subject for a few days, then bring it up again. She wanted to come out as a lesbian and have a full-on relationship with ME, but I kept telling her no. I think it was the added pressure that threw me into the arms of Olivia.

Olivia was the party girl in the group. Next to her was our honorary male lesbian friend Henry. He was also American and on the nights that we didn't want to go out, he'd always be up for accompanying Olivia to one club or the next. She was known for her partying, one of the main contributing factors in her ex-husband being awarded full custody of her child. She couldn't help herself; it was as though she was constantly running away from something. Every one of us had tried the occasional puff of marijuana when we travelled to one country or the next and got a good hook up, but Olivia was hardcore. She'd taken cocaine and many other recreational drugs. She led a dangerous life, but she was an amazing person and we all loved her, well, at least I did. Her honesty was uncanny; she couldn't care whether you'd be offended, she'd always tell the truth whether you asked for it or not.

It was after 11pm when Henry messaged me and asked me to join him and Olivia at a local bar. Elsa was lying next to me in bed fast asleep, while I laid awake thinking of how I was going to get out of whatever it was that was going on with her. I was never alone anymore. When she wasn't there, Lorelei was; and I was being suffocated.

To both mine and Henry's surprise, I agreed to go meet them at the bar. When I got there Olivia was having a good time as she always does, socialising and mixing with every human being possible. When Abba's Dancing Queen came on she came to dance in front of me. Between singing and dancing, she often leaned forward to touch me and when the song was finished, she grabbed me by my arm and motioned us towards the bathroom.

"Why are you such a grouch tonight Izzie?"

"Huh, what do you mean?"

"I mean just that, you look miserable."

"Oh, do I? I didn't realise. You know what, maybe I should just go home. It seemed like a good idea at the time but obviously, it wasn't. I shouldn't have come."

I walked out of the bathroom and she followed me.

"Henry, I think I'm gonna go. This was a mistake. I'm exhausted, and I have work to do tomorrow."

"Come on Izzie don't leave," Henry shouted over the music, blasting my eardrum.

"Sorry darling, I'll make it up to you this weekend." I kissed him on the cheek and Olivia pulled me by the arm again, this time towards the exit door.

We exited the bar and she led me down the street. Less than a block down from the bar, she dragged me into an alleyway and stuck her tongue in my mouth. Before you knew it, I was pressing her against the wall doing all kinds of things to her and once again I was where I wanted to be, doing what I wanted to do. Olivia was the queen of one-night stands, so I imagined it would all blow off smoothly. We'd wake up in the morning as grown women who understood the need to get one off and just have sex for the sake of having sex.

When she came I removed my fingers, pulled her skirt down and wiped her juices off on the inside of my jacket. I walked her back to the bar, kissed her goodbye and walked home. I was disappointed to find Elsa still sleeping in my bed, completely oblivious to the fact that I had gone out.

*****

The nagging from Elsa didn't stop and I still had no intentions of taking her virginity, I didn't think I deserved it and I didn't hide that fact from her. When she didn't stop pushing, I began to care less about the fact that I wanted to fuck anyone I wanted without her finding out. I knew for a fact that I didn't want to hurt her, but she wasn't getting the message and I was utterly frustrated. I needed a break from everyone, so I took a trip to Paris all on my own for the weekend.

I told no one I was going: I just left. It was a well-needed break. Had it not been for the Elsa thing, I would have been perfectly fine. I wasn't connected to Lorelei and I wasn't particularly worried about not committing to her, we both knew that I could never settle down with her. We just didn't mesh outside of the bedroom, or the bathroom, well you know what I mean. Elsa, on the other hand, I really cared about, but I couldn't give her what she wanted and I didn't know how to get her to understand.

While in Paris, I met a Kyrgyzstan national named Jyrgal who was living in London. It was her who approached me while I was waiting in line to take the tour of the Eifel Tower. She was quite brazen.

"I don't know if you know this yet, but you will soon be my lifetime companion. We'll have a house filled with children and the most exciting life traveling the world together."

I couldn't control myself and I began to laugh uncontrollably.

"I know you're laughing now, but you won't be once you realise I was telling the truth."

"Okay then prophetess," I mocked.

'You'll see. I promise."

It was our first encounter. When the tour was over, I came to find her waiting at the exit. I found her strange standing there, but I was also intrigued. We spent a few hours together walking around Paris getting to know each other. She was almost 20 years my senior and was representing her consulate in London. The thing that bothered me the most was the fact that she was in an eight years relationship, but was busy prowling the streets of Paris. Even I knew it was a recipe for disaster. It was nice getting to know her, but I had no intentions of being caught in a love triangle. I didn't escape to Paris for the weekend to be bogged down with more problems. So, though I enjoyed her company I steered clear of sending her any mixed signals about my intentions. She asked for my number and I decided there was no harm in sharing it and gave it to her.

Returning to my apartment, I found both Olivia and Elsa waiting for me. Elsa called her over because "she was worried about me".

"Hi, didn't expect anyone would be here."

"Well hi to you too. We've all been worried sick. Where have you been?" Elsa said.

"You all realise I am grown right? Like, I am a grown responsible woman who can go away for the weekend."

"Why are you so hostile?" Olivia contributed. I imagined if she said I sounded hostile, then I was indeed communicating that.

I adjusted my tone. "Sorry about that, just tired. I needed a bit of a break. I didn't mean to make anyone worry."

"So where did you go then?" Oliva probed.

"Nowhere special, just up to Rothenberg."

"Oh, interesting and you didn't want any of us to go with?" Elsa's face made it obvious she knew I was lying.

"I didn't want to bother anyone, plus I needed some time alone."

"Well I suppose now that you're home safe we can all get on with our lives. Come on then Elsa, we should go." She sounded irritated with me, but I didn't quite care.

I wanted them gone from my apartment. As usual, Elsa obeyed her command and the two of them left. I could tell she wanted to stay, but I

wanted my apartment to myself, so I made it clear
that it was okay for her to follow Olivia's lead.

* * * * *

I tried spending less time with the ladies and tried
not to get too friendly with anyone. Time on my
own meant that I had time to think more about
Puteri, but I preferred the heartache over all the
drama that Elsa was bringing into my life. Now
that I had fucked Olivia too, I was worried that
they'd sit down and have a heart to heart and
she'd end up broken-hearted. That thought alone
was slowly driving me crazy. I talked a lot with
Jyrgal on the phone and tried hard not to
entertain her sexual innuendos. I imagined her
partner finding out about me and possibly
humiliating me on Facebook as a homewrecker;
public humiliation over social media was quickly

becoming a trend and so I tried to avoid it at all costs.

For sex, there was Lorelei who would show up when I wanted her to and then there was the ever-growing opportunity of a one-night stand when I went on a night out. These were options far better than becoming entangled in an affair with Jyrgal, plus the thought of being the other woman was just not appealing to me. Olivia also became a bit of a constant for late night rendezvous and the good thing about it was that she'd never call me to talk outside of being friends or expected anything from me that I couldn't deliver.

* * * * *

I spent the day dodging calls from Elsa. She wanted to spend the weekend together, but I wasn't up for it. I tried hard to tell her I didn't want to continue doing whatever it was that we were doing. I even arranged a blind date for her with a guy from work who was just as good a person as she was and we'd been work friends since I started there. He was a churchgoer, a real sweetheart and single, so I arranged for the two of them to meet. Elsa didn't take to it though; she wanted what she wanted.

Just after 9pm, there was someone downstairs ringing my doorbell. Out of fear it was Elsa, I decided not to pick up the intercom, but the person kept buzzing and eventually I decided to answer the door. I was right, it was Elsa.

"Where were you, let me up."

"Sorry was taking a nap." I buzzed her in.

Against my will, I was huddled on the sofa with Elsa watching TV. After several episodes of Friends, we were still huddled together on the sofa. I didn't want to go to bed, I didn't want to wake up to Elsa eating my pussy or to feel her pulling me closer to her halfway between being asleep and awake. I wanted my bed to myself.

There was a buzz on the intercom after 1am and I imagined someone had buzzed the wrong apartment, so I rolled over, looked at the time and decided to ignore the bell. I was drifting off to sleep again when there was a knock at the door and it was no regular knock, I thought it was the police. I sprung up from the bed waking Elsa as well.

"What's going on?" she questioned.

"I don't know, someone's at the door." I stumbled across the room to grab my robe. She followed me to the door.

She peered through the peephole and recognised Olivia standing there. "It's Olivia," she whispered. "What is she doing here?"

"I don't know, is she drunk?" I pretended this was something completely new to me.

She opened the door and Olivia opened her coat. She was stark naked underneath it, just as she'd shown up many times for one of our late-night escapades. My heart dropped, I wanted the fucking earth to open up and swallow me whole.

* * * * *

Olivia being the type of woman she is didn't have an issue with whatever was going on between me and Elsa, but Elsa, as I had predicted, was broken hearted. She wanted nothing to do with me and I completely understood. When I left for England she was the only friend who wasn't present at my leaving party. I didn't quite mind in the sense that I was happy that it was over, and I was leaving. I completed both my masters and got a job working for a corporate in London. It didn't hurt that I was going to be close to Jyrgal who I'd gotten to know more and was again starting a new chapter in my life. Moving from country to country became somewhat appealing, especially when I needed the escape.

When I wrote my letter to Elsa, it was Olivia who I sent it to, for her to forward to her for me. The two remained close, rightly so. Olivia and I stayed in touch but since getting married, communications had become less so when I sent her the letter for Elsa, she read it before passing it on. In true Olivia form, she turned up in London weeks later to do what we do best. I soon realised that I was recycling my sexual encounters. Since leaving my wife, I hadn't met anyone new outside of my therapist and that was just sex; well work and sex. Anyway, what was meant to be a step in a new direction was turning up to be a recycling project. I wanted to merely apologise and move on whether or not I was forgiven, but here I was rehashing flames where they should have remained dead.

# The final chapter?

It was Jyrgal whom I married. I genuinely do not want to get into it. That is a story for another time and what a fucking story it will be. It was an absolute nightmare and I'm still surprised that I'm getting past it. This was my ultimate fuckup in life and after four long years, I was happy to escape all of it.

This is where my therapist and my task came in. In the process of trying to recover and heal, I decided to take things a step further and right my wrongs. Hence, I didn't just want to write my letters and burn them. The ones who I had hurt badly, needed to know that I was sorry for whatever pain I had caused them. I wanted to fix whatever I could. I knew for a fact that after Jyrgal, I was going to find it hard to trust anyone again and I wondered whether I had left anyone

in that state. I didn't expect to end up back in bed
or any form of intimate relationship with any of
them, but we often get more than we bargain for,
isn't it.

I knew that one of the most difficult letters I was
going to write was to Puteri, but I had to at least
try. I didn't know what had become of her, never
checked but have always wondered. I didn't dear
google her out of fear that I'd pursue her and
cause her more pain than I had originally.

A few weeks after getting married, a huge
bouquet had turned up at my work with a note
that read, *I'm happy you are happy.* It didn't say
who they were from and the flower shop refused
to disclose who had ordered them, claiming the
person paid cash and didn't give a name. With it
being from the most expensive florist in all of
London, I assumed it was from her but quickly

put the thought out of my mind. I didn't want to think that she was a bystander in my life. That she'd watched the woman she wanted to spend the rest of her life with pledge her life to someone else.

It took me quite a long time before accepting Jyrgal's proposal. I do think it was out of fear that I finally accepted, and it was fear that kept me in the marriage and fear that made me escape.

In my letter to Puteri, I told her how the cruellest thing I had done to date was walk out on her and that I couldn't shake it. I told her that I thought of her every single day and hoped she'd met the woman of her dreams and settled down like she wanted to. I told her about the adventures I'd have over the last six years and how I'd take it all back if I could take away whatever pain I had caused her. For the first time since leaving her, I pursued Puteri. It wasn't hard. I rang up her company in Kuala Lumpur and spoke with a receptionist.

"Hello, is that you Miss Isabel?"

"Yes, who is this?"

"It's me Maeena. I work at the reception desk now Madam.'

"Oh, hello Maeena, how are you? Good to hear your voice!" I wasn't sure who I was speaking with and hoped that I didn't give it away.

"I'm okay Madam, thank you. How are you?"

"I'm great too, thanks. Maeena, is....."

"Aw yes madam wait one moment, I'll transfer the call."

"No no no, wait Maeena, don't do that. I was just checking."

"Aw Miss Isabel Madam, please, I'll put you through to Madam. She's not okay Miss Isabel. She would want to hear from you. We were all waiting for you to call."

I was flabbergasted, I dropped the phone in a panic. Whoever Maeena was she seemed to know an awful lot, and this meant that she knew the monster that was me on the other end of the phone.

Another couple of weeks passed when I received another bunch of flowers at my office with another note and no name, I'm here when you're ready. I was sure now that it was Puteri who had originally sent the flowers and her who had sent these as well. But what did she mean? Had she forgiven me? I decided to send my letter to the only email address I had for her. It was a Yahoo account she claimed she had created only for me.

I imagined she had closed it down, but was relieved when the email was not returned undelivered.

The day went by and though I checked every possible second, there was no response to the email. All kind of thoughts went through my head. Why did she send me roses if only to ignore me when I reached out? Were the flowers even from her? Why was she ignoring me? Did she read my letter and did it make her angry? Did it bring up old wounds that she didn't want to have to face? I began second-guessing myself and wondered whether I had made a mistake.

Night came and there was still no response from her. In my apartment, I laid on the bedroom floor looking at the London skies wishing I could take it all back. I played Bruno Mars talking to the moon and wailed. I didn't want to hurt her, and I imagined I had done just that. Who was I to walk in and out of her life as I pleased? No wonder she wanted nothing to do with me: no wonder she was ignoring me. I wanted her to forget that I existed, but at the same time, I wanted to call her. I wanted to be the one that soothed whatever pain she was feeling. Laying there on the floor, it dawned on me that I never really dealt with what had happened between us. I didn't give her an explanation even though she deserved one. I also never gave myself time to dissect what had conspired between us or how I had walked away from everything and just jumped into a new life. I realised that my wild and reckless behaviour was my way of avoiding facing any of it.

Without thinking, I sent a message to Nurin who had given me a proper telling off only months earlier. Surprisingly she was different this time around.

"I suppose it was only a matter of time that you asked. Have you tried calling her?"

"What do you mean, I don't have a direct number for her."

"You do, she's not changed anything. She still has the same old number and lives in the same apartment. Still has the apartment in Bangkok too. She bought it after you left."

"Are you serious? Why did she do that?"

"Until the other day when I lost my temper with you I didn't get it, but as you've held on to her, she's held on to you. You didn't want to carry on a conversation with me, but it meant you had some sort of connection to her. That's the only reason you put up with me."

"Nurin, come on."

"There's no need to hide how you feel Izzie. I understand completely. You should get in touch with Pu though, it would do you both a lot of good. All of Kuala Lumpur knows she is pining over you and quite frankly we are all tired of seeing it now."

"Nurin, I'm really sorry for how I've treated you. I really am."

"You've already apologised to me, there's no need to be sorry. I should have treated you better, but I know we were just not meant to be. Whatever happened between you and my sister, try to work it out. You've been away for years and she's not dated anyone so it's obvious she's waiting for you. It can be fixed so try and fix it."

"What? Is she not in a relationship?"

"Don't sound so surprised. My sister loves me, and she still took you from me. That's a different kind of love. What did you expect? She's not been with anyone since."

When Nurin said that I felt my heart shatter into a thousand pieces. The life I had lived was undeserving of the kind of woman Puteri was. She deserved better. I didn't want to bother her, but I also didn't want to leave her alone in the state she was in.

It all began to make sense, I had been through so much in my marriage because of the pain I had caused her. It was karma.

* * * * *

I waited impatiently for 9am in Kuala Lumpur. If everything had stayed the same with Puteri, she was going to turn up at the office at around

8:30am, have her cup of coffee and prepare for work at 9am. She never took meetings for the first hour each morning. She wanted to ensure that everything was running smoothly in the office before diving into it. She said it was her way of ensuring that she was a part of her team and not just a boss figure to her staff. Though she had different managers for different departments, she engaged with staff at different levels and tried not to create a wedge between her and them. It was one of the qualities I loved about her.

The time came and I decided to call her office. I didn't want to call her direct line, I needed a buffer between us. I wanted her to be told I was calling so that she'd have the chance to decide if she wanted to take my call. I didn't want her to feel pressured into talking with me.

"Good morning Megat's Enterprise, you're through to Aqil. How may I direct your call?"

"Oh hello Aqil," it was a voice and name I recognised. He'd been working there when I was there too.

"Isabel Madam?"

The sense of familiarity brought me a sense of relief. "Yes, it's me Aqil."

"Madam are you in Kuala Lumpur?"

"Unfortunately, no. Sorry Aqil, is Puteri in?"

"Isabel Madam, Puteri Madam is not here today Madam. She's been off work for a while now. Do you want to leave a message with her PA Madam?"

"It's okay Aqil. I will try again."

"I will tell Madam that you called."

"No need Aqil, nice talking with you."

"And you Miss Isabel Madam."

I felt defeated. I gave up. There was still no response to my email, I didn't want to assume anymore. I gave up.

# You might have guessed

I wasn't in the mood for work but pulled myself together and made my way to the tube station anyway. I felt naked, as though everyone could see my wounds. I would have much preferred to be wrapped up under my duvet weeping than be seen out in public. In my mind, the cinematic recording of my life kept playing over and over again, with each scene including Puteri. I wanted to reach out and touch her. I wanted to hold her. Ours was the relationship I wanted to recycle and hold on to. I wanted to keep my promise; to be there when her business deal was completed. I wanted to kiss her forehead again and tell her that I'd be there and mean it. I wanted to trust that if she could have come to my rescue she would have. I wanted to trust that she wasn't having an affair, that she was doing what she claimed to be doing.

* * * * *

Before noon I got a call from my divorce lawyer.

"Thanks for the payment. I believe that it should cover everything that Jyrgal is asking for, our fees and the court fees. If anything, I'll...."

"Wait what payment? What are you talking about?"

"What do you mean what payment? The one you made out to us. It's Hayleigh Wigan from Pollards and Associates."

"I know who it is, but I haven't made a payment. I don't know what you're talking about. I don't have the kind of money Jyrgal is asking for and even if I did, I wouldn't pay her a dime. I'd rather fight her in court."

"Is it okay if I call you back? A payment went into our account yesterday and used your reference."

"Yes, please do that. I didn't make a payment. I would need to sell my flat to be able to pay that kind of money to Jyrgal and she knows that. I do not intend on paying her a dime."

"I completely understand, leave it with me and I'll get back to you as soon as I can."

It was puzzling at first, but as soon as I hung up from the lawyer it clicked. The only person I know who could pay £250,000 over without feeling the pinch was Puteri. But how would she have known about the divorce? How did she know anything for that matter? It all clicked. She must have been watching me, she must know what I have been up to. I didn't post anything about getting married on social media and I didn't change my name; so how did she know?

I began to feel ill and my stomach churned. I was going to be sick. I pulled out the bin from under my desk just in time. I felt ill, sick to my stomach. There was no way I could face her now. I decided to call my lawyer back because I needed confirmation.

"Can you tell me how much the payment was for?"

"It was £300,000. But Isabel the reference used was yours. The payment was made by a company in Malaysia. Are you sure you don't know who made this payment?"

"My mistake, yes I do know. Sorry about the mix-up."

* * * * *

On the ride from Piccadilly Circus to Paddington, I kept mistaking people for Puteri. I could see her everywhere. I didn't understand what was going on though, why had she still not responded to my email and why did she pay the money over for my divorce. Granted, I wanted to divorce this woman as soon as I possibly could, but I didn't want her to get a dime. I'd been the one to bear the financial brunt of everything in our relationship. I shouldn't have to continue. Anyway, why was she helping me, sending me flowers telling me she's ready when I am but not responding to my email! It was frustrating and painful all at the same time.

* * * * *

On Wednesday evening I received a text message on my work mobile advising that the office would only be opened at 11am due to a fire drill that the council was going to be carrying out on Thursday. I was relieved. I didn't want to go into work, but figured it would have been better than staying in with my walls and my thoughts. Jyrgal had refused to give me my dog, so I was completely alone at the flat. She had done a great job at keeping me from people so the once social butterfly I had been had died and I no longer entertained friends or hung out much.

After the text, a call came in from my therapist. I had completely forgotten about my appointment. This was becoming a habit, because I hadn't shown up the last two weeks either. It was for more reasons than one. I was now pining over Puteri and didn't want to talk to her about it, plus I didn't want to fuck her or anyone else for that matter. I decided to take her call this time.

"Hey, sorry I completely forgot that I was meant to see you today. Mind if I take a rain check?"

"I'm sorry Isabel, but I won't be able to continue with our sessions."

"What? What do you mean? What's happened?"

"Isabel, I'm so sorry. I haven't done well by you as my client. I crossed the line and by doing so, I have gotten in the way of your therapy."

"Come on Gabrielle, what are you on about? I'm a grown woman I can take care of myself."

"I'll forward an email to you with some options. Anyone on the list will be good and I'd recommend working with any of them."

"Will you cut the crap? I'm coming over now."

She hung up the phone. I called a few times, but there was no answer. I was halfway through the door when it dawned on me that I couldn't just show up: that it was possible that her husband had found out about us and asked her to end it. I decided not to go over there.

I kept checking but there was still nothing from Puteri. I decided to send her an email.

*I know I can't take any of it back. God knows I wish I could, but I can't. You may never forgive me and that's okay but even a "don't bother me" would help.*

I hit the send button and the email was gone. It didn't sum up what I wanted to say, but I didn't want to send another never-ending email that she wouldn't respond to.

Sleep evaded me and before long, it was morning. I was only meant to do my usual 5k on the treadmill, but was well into the 16k going on 17 when I felt the burn on my heel. When I stopped the treadmill to check, my feet were bleeding. I was badly bruised and too deeply wrapped up in my thoughts to feel or notice.

I soaked my feet and dressed them. Luckily it was the middle of summer and a warm day out that I could wear a maxi dress with a pair of sandals that didn't go around my ankles. I decided to walk to the office. Travelling from my apartment on Clifton Place it was a lovely walk over to the office on Peter Street. The sun wasn't too warm, and I needed to get away from the bustle and heat of the underground.

Arriving at the office, I found my colleague Imran making his way in as well.

"Izzieeeee!"

I smiled at him, whenever he called me it was always as though he was doing a sing-song. "Hi Imran."

"Do you mind walking with me to the tube station? I think I lost my wallet there."

"Sorry about that. Come on, why not, we still have about half an hour anyway." I didn't mind; the thought of being at work wasn't appealing.

As we walked we talked. Imran asked quite a few questions about my life and how I'd ended up in England. It was a bit strange as he wasn't an inquisitive guy which is why we got along. Without knowing, I found myself answering all his questions. I gave little information, but still tried to answer all of them without sounding condescending.

He didn't get his wallet, so we made our way back to the office. Strolling slowly, making conversations.

Everyone we passed in the building seemed to have been busy with work already. We still had a few minutes left, but I suppose they were more eager to get started than I was.

"Izzie, you reckon you have a strong heart love?" He asked, holding me by both shoulders and bending forward to look me in my eyes.

"What are you on about, come on let's go to work." I tried to move, but Imran held me in place.

All of a sudden, he was hugging me. "Wherever life takes you, please remember me. You were a breath of fresh air around here."

"Is something wrong with you? Have you got cancer? Why does it sound like you are saying goodbye to me?"

"No, I don't have cancer Izzie. I just simply appreciate you. That's all."

I was becoming aware that time was passing by. No one from our floor had passed us on the way, so we were possibly the only two people left to get on the floor. "Okay Imran, I care about you too, but you can't get rid of me. At least not for a while. Come on, let's get to work."

Imran opened the door for me to walk through. I looked back to say thank you and for a moment I thought I got a glimpse of Puteri: then, as though my mind registered what I really saw, I was forced to refocus my attention ahead of me.

She was standing there, she was right in front of me. She began to walk towards me. At first, I couldn't move. I tried to walk, but my legs didn't move. Then as if a fire had been lit beneath my feet, I sprang into her arms crashing into the flowers she held in her hand. I kissed her and touched her and kissed her again. I didn't know if she was real.

"I'm sorry about everything my PuBear. I'm sorry I walked out on you, on us. I'm sorry for ....." she broke my words with her kiss.

"I'm the one who should be sorry. I'm sorry for not coming after you, but can we talk about this later, everyone is watching."

I soon realised that everyone from the office was standing there watching us, even the managers. I was embarrassed for a mere second, but no one could get in the way of what I was feeling. Though unsure of what was to come for us, I was happy to be standing in the same place as Puteri. She reached into her pocket and took out the ring she had proposed to me with years before.

"Will you do me the honour of wearing your ring?" Before I could respond, she placed it on my finger. There was a huge uproar in the office and everyone was cheering and clapping. "I love you Izzie, and I will love you until my last breath." She whispered.

* * * * * * *

Hello friends,

I hope you enjoyed this book! The follow up is coming next June and I can't wait to share it with you. Look out for "Puteri's version of things"!

TAMARiND HiLL
.PRESS